Boys Town, Nebraska

Of COURSE It's a Big Deal!

A Story about Learning to React Calmly and Appropriately

Written by **Bryan Smith**

Illustrated by **Lisa M. Griffin**

For Puster Elementary teachers. Thank you for helping your students learn to react appropriately.

Of Course It's a Big Deal!
Text and Illustrations Copyright © 2017 by Father Flanagan's Boys' Home
ISBN: 978-1-944882-11-2

Published by the Boys Town Press
14100 Crawford St.
Boys Town, NE 68010

For a Boys Town Press catalog, call **1-800-282-6657**
or visit our website: **BoysTownPress.org**

Publisher's Cataloging-in-Publication Data

Names: Smith, Bryan (Bryan Kyle), 1978- author. | Griffin, Lisa M. (Lisa Middleton), 1972- illustrator.

Title: Of course it's a big deal! : a story about learning to react calmly and appropriately / written by Bryan Smith ; illustrated by Lisa M. Griffin.

Description: Boys Town, NE : Boys Town Press, [2017] | Audience: grades K-6. | Summary: Braden delivers drama to every minor misunderstanding, grievance and annoyance in his life! Will he learn to keep his cool in the face of disappointment, or will every discouraging moment send him into an emotional meltdown? See what lessons he learns in this fast-paced story about the perils of overreacting and losing self-control.--Publisher.

Identifiers: 978-1-944882-11-2

Subjects: LCSH: Self-control in children--Juvenile fiction. | Emotions in children--Juvenile fiction. | Stress in children--Juvenile fiction. | Anxiety in children--Juvenile fiction. | Calmness--Juvenile fiction. | Self-reliance in children--Juvenile fiction. | Attitude change in children-- Juvenile fiction. | Child psychology--Juvenile fiction. | Interpersonal relations in children--Juvenile fiction. | Children--Life skills guides--Juvenile fiction. | CYAC: Self-control--Fiction. | Emotions--Fiction. | Stress--Fiction. | Anxiety--Fiction. | Calmness--Fiction. | Self-reliance-- Fiction. | Change (Psychology)--Fiction. | Interpersonal relations--Fiction. | Conduct of life-- Fiction. | BISAC: JUVENILE FICTION / Social Themes / Emotions & Feelings. | JUVENILE FICTION / Social Themes / Self-Esteem & Self-Reliance. | EDUCATION / Counseling / General.

Classification: LCC: PZ7.S643366 O4 2017 | DDC: [Fic]--dc23

Printed in the United States
10 9 8 7 6 5 4 3 2

Boys Town Press is the publishing division of Boys Town, a national organization serving children and families.

You see, my parents just don't get it. They must have forgotten what it's like to be a kid.

3

But it doesn't matter, because there's no way when **THEY** were kids that they had to deal with **ANYTHING** like what I have to deal with.

I mean, they seriously act like the stuff that bugs me isn't a big deal, as if they know what is or is not a big deal!

They can't! They're parents! They haven't been kids in like

100 years... like since the pilgrims!

4

Anyway, here's the thing. I was doing great behaving myself at school, so my parents decided to take my little brother and me to the Fun Zone.

The place has bumper cars, putt-putt golf, videogames, and lots of other cool stuff.

And I couldn't **WAIT** to drive a go-cart for the first time!

When we got there, I ran straight to the go-cart track. As soon as the guy who worked there opened the gate to let us in, I immediately ran to the yellow go-cart.

Then I heard, *"WHOA there!"* I turned around and the worker said,

"Who's going to drive for you?"

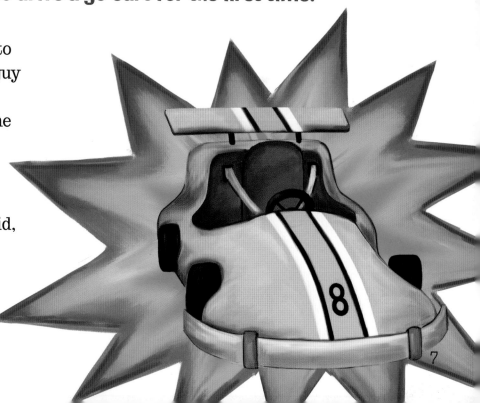

"Um, no one," I told him.

And that's when it happened.

The worst words I could ever imagine came out of his mouth. *"I'm sorry, but you aren't*

TALL

enough to drive yourself."

I stood there, stunned.
I mean, seriously, he **HAD**
to be joking, right? Obviously,
he had never seen me play my
race car videogame at home.

I ran to Mom to tell her about
this because I just knew she
would let me drive myself.

Boy was I **WRONG!**

"Sorry, Braden, a rule is a rule. And we need to follow the rules," declared Mom.

I was shocked! Her words came at me like they were said in slow motion.
So I shouted, "Well that's a dumb rule, and I think you and this guy just hate kids!"

"Kid, it's not that big of a deal. You can ride
with someone else," said the worker dude.

It IS a **BIG DEAL!**

"**I hate this place!**

I just want to get out of here!"

I then ran off and sat on
a sticky wooden bench.

Dad stayed in the go-cart line and rode with my brother Blake. Mom had quietly followed me and then sat next to me. When Dad and Blake finished, they went to play putt-putt. I looked at Mom and said, "I thought we were going home."

"No. Your trip here is ruined only if you let it be that way. I think you might be overreacting a little. Don't you think?"

"Of course not!" I said. "You just don't get it. You don't know what it's like to be a kid."

11

Smiling, Mom said, "You know, it's been a while since I was a kid. But I used to have a hard time staying calm when things didn't go my way, too. *That is until your Grandpa sat me down and told me about his plan on how to do it.*"

12

**Here's the thing. I love my Grandpa.
He's the coolest old guy on the planet.**

And he gets it!
He really gets it!

So even though I didn't want to hear anything but the words, "Sorry, Braden, it was all a mistake. Go ahead and drive the go-cart," I **WAS** a little bit interested in hearing what Grandpa had said.

I sighed and quietly asked,
"So, what's his plan?"

"Grandpa showed me four easy steps to staying calm. You just have to be willing to stop what you're doing and try them out," explained Mom.

4 STEPS to Reacting calmly

The steps Grandpa taught me are:

#1 Calm down. You can take deep breaths or count to 10.

#2 Think of a way to make the situation better.

#3 Try it out.

#4 If nothing works, or if you can't figure out what to do, get help.

"I am not happy you shouted out those things at the track and ran away, but I'm proud that you eventually found a quiet spot and settled down. What did you do to help calm yourself down?"

"I have no idea."

Mom replied, "Could you have just walked away without shouting?"

"Maybe, but it's hard," I said.

"You're right, but it's the right thing to do."

Mom told me she likes to take deep breaths and count to 10 to calm down while Grandpa likes to close his eyes and think of a happy place. When it comes to the second step, she said I needed to think about ways I could have handled the situation better.

"I know," I said. **"I could sit on top of your shoulders to make me tall enough to drive the go-cart!"**

"Do you really think that's going to work?"

16

"Probably not. Well, I suppose I could just not ride the go-carts until I'm tall enough."

"Sure, but don't you think it would still be fun to ride along with someone who is tall enough?"

"Maybe," I said.

"You could ride with Dad or me."

I took a deep breath and thought for a minute. Maybe that wouldn't be too awful... at least I'd get to ride, right?

"Can I take a ride with each of you?"

"Sure! But that can only happen if you stay calm and try your new way of making the situation better. And just think, now you get to ride twice."

Actually, that sounded really great!

We went and found Dad and Blake, and we all rode the go-carts twice. The rest of the day was a blast.

13 Okay, so maybe I did overreact a little bit.

19

After we got home that night, **I was SUPER EXCITED to watch baseball with Dad.**

Sometimes we wear our jerseys and pretend we're really at the game. I asked Dad if he wanted me to grab his jersey. Mom overheard me and said it was too late to watch the game. I had to get ready for bed.

"Whaaat??!

I wasn't even asking you!" I said.

"Hey, that's no way to talk to your mother," Dad snapped. "Looks like you WON'T be watching the game tonight. You need to head straight to your room."

"Can I at least watch ONE inning with you?"

"The only thing you can watch is the way you talk to your mom."

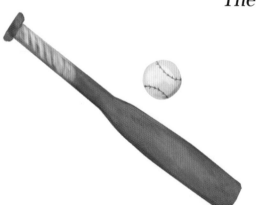

As I walked to my room, Dad turned on the baseball game and I mumbled to myself,

"That's NOT fair!"

In my room, I took a few deep breaths to calm down and thought of a plan to make the situation better.

Then it came to me!

If I can't watch it, neither can Dad.
I ran straight downstairs and
threw a blanket over the TV!

When I saw the look on Dad's face, I quickly knew it was a

BAD, BAD plan.

He marched me right back to my room, and I lost TV privileges for a **WHOLE WEEK!**

Later, Dad came back to my room and said he was disappointed by what I did.

*"Braden, overreacting does not help you or anyone out. We need to come up with a **PLAN**."*

I told Dad about the steps Mom talked to me about. I told him that when I was sent to bed, I calmed myself by taking deep breaths and then came up with the idea to make the situation better... my blanket-over-the-TV plan.

"Did it really make anything better?" Dad asked. "It seems to me you made the situation worse."

23

"Yeah, I guess you're right." I confessed.

"Now, what else could you have done to make the situation better?"

"I should have just gone to bed and not done anything."

"Maybe, but I think that would have made the situation worse for you. *It didn't have to be such a big deal, did it? What if* you had suggested we watch the game tomorrow night?"

"Dad, I'm pretty sure the players wouldn't stop the game for us."

"*Ha!* That's not what I meant," he chuckled. "I could record it."

"That's a great idea! Why can't I think of things like that?"

"You can. It just takes practice. The key is to remain calm so you can think
of good ways to help make a situation better."

A few days later, we celebrated Mom's birthday at a restaurant. For dessert, we ordered her a huge ice cream sundae with candles on it. The whole time my brother and I stared at the sundae like two hungry vultures. Mom must have noticed because she slid the sundae over to us and said we could share it.

As I grabbed my spoon, my nasty brother licked the top off the sundae.
Ugh! **I wanted to smash that sundae in his face!**

But then I realized I had to show my parents that I wouldn't overreact. I closed my eyes like Grandpa said and thought of a happy place. I pretended I was swimming in a pool of ice cream! When I opened my eyes, I wasn't so mad anymore and I had a solution.

STEP #1

STEP #2

STEP #3

"Dad, can I please get my own sundae?"

"Sorry, no. We don't have time to get another one."

"But Blake licked the whole thing.

That's gross!"

I felt myself getting angry again, so I tried my best to stay calm by taking a deep breath. If I shouted, whined, or did something I shouldn't, I'd get punished again. I'll just ask Dad about this later.

STEP #4

In the car, I kept quiet. Right before we got home, Dad pulled into the parking lot of our neighborhood grocery store and said, "Braden, I need you to come inside with me."

"Okay," I said, wondering why he couldn't go by himself.

Once in the store, Dad walked straight to the frozen food section. There, he opened up the refrigerator door, grabbed a huge tub of vanilla ice cream, and said, *"You did a great job of staying calm when things didn't go your way at the restaurant. Think this will work for a sundae at home?"*

I slapped my face to make sure I wasn't dreaming of a happy place.

"Oh, yeah!"

Dad even let me get sprinkles, chocolate syrup, and whipped cream!

After we got home, Mom, Dad, and I got to eat our own sundaes. But not Blake because he made a bad choice when he licked Mom's birthday sundae!

Vanilla

Chocolat

erry

When Dad told my brother he couldn't have a sundae, Blake stuck out his tongue and knocked the sprinkles to the ground.

I turned to Mom and Dad and said,

"**Sheesh,** what an over-reactor! It's not a big deal!"

When children don't get what they want or expect, they often get upset and angry. Reacting calmly and appropriately during these times is an important skill for children to learn and use to be successful at home, school, and with others.

Here are some tips and suggestions parents and teachers can use to teach kids how to **react calmly and appropriately:**

1. **Point out when you see someone else overreact,** and ask your children what they would have done in that situation.

2. **Teach children relaxation strategies** to use when they feel like they might overreact (count to ten, deep breathing, think of a happy place, etc.).

3. **Have children write down their feelings.** This can help them learn how to express their emotions in an appropriate way.

4. **Take care of your basic needs.** People who are tired or hungry tend to overreact more easily.

5. **Teach children** it's okay to ask for help.

6. **Praise children** when they react calmly and appropriately.

7. **Be a role model for children.** Be sure to express your thoughts in a calm manner during times when you feel like you might overreact.

8. **Brainstorm with children** situations where people might tend to overreact and role play how to handle these situations appropriately.

For more parenting information, visit boystown.org/parenting.

BOYS TOWN® Parenting

Boys Town Press Featured Titles
Kid-friendly books to teach social skills

Executive FuNction

What Were You **Thinking?**

978-1-934490-85-3

Downloadable Activities
Go to BoysTownPress.org to download.

My Day Is **Ruined!**
A Story for Teaching Flexible Thinking
Written by Bryan Smith
Illustrated by Lisa M. Griffin

978-1-944882-04-4

Of COURSE It's a **Big Deal!**
A Story about Learning to React Calmly and Appropriately
Written by Bryan Smith
Illustrated by Lisa M. Griffin

978-1-944882-11-2

It Was Just **Right Here!**
Written by Bryan Smith
Illustrated by Lisa M. Griffin

978-1-944882-20-4

When I couldn't get OVER it, I learned to **Start Acting Differently**
A story about managing SADness
Written by Bryan Smith
Illustrated by Lisa M. Griffin

978-1-944882-22-8

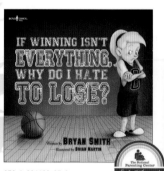

Is There an **App for That?**
Written by Bryan Smith
Illustrated by Katie Wish

Hailey Discovers HAPPiness through Self-Acceptance

978-1-934490-74-7

Without Limits
dream • connect • soar

Downloadable Activities
Go to BoysTownPress.org to download.

MINDSET MATTERS
Written by Bryan Smith
Illustrated by Lisa Griffin

978-1-944882-12-9

Kindness Counts
a story for teaching random acts of kindness
Written by Bryan Smith
Illustrated by Brian Martin

978-1-944882-01-3

IF WINNING ISN'T **EVERYTHING, WHY DO I HATE TO LOSE?**
Written by BRYAN SMITH
Illustrated by BRIAN MARTIN

The National Parenting Center
Seal of Approval

978-1-934490-85-3

BOYS TOWN Press®

For information on Boys Town, its Education Model, Common Sense Parenting®, and training programs:
boystowntraining.org | boystown.org/parenting
training@BoysTown.org | 1-800-545-5771

For parenting and educational books and other resources:
BoysTownPress.org
btpress@BoysTown.org | 1-800-282-6657